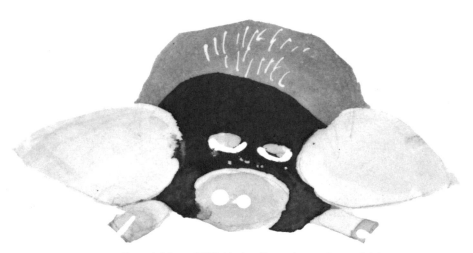

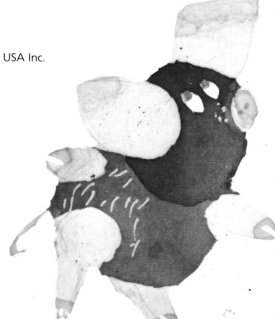

Library of Congress Cataloging in Publication Data
Three little pigs.
The Three little pigs.
Summary: Relates the adventures of the three little pigs
who leave home to try their luck in the world.
[1. Folklore. 2. Pigs–Fiction] I. Reinl, Edda, Ill.
PZ8.1.T383 1983  398.2'4529734 [E]      83-8256
ISBN 0-907234-32-1

Edda Reinl

# THE 3 LITTLE PIGS

PICTURE BOOK STUDIO USA

Once upon a time,
there was a mother pig who had three piglets.
The three little pigs played and ate and slept every day,
and soon they were all grown up.
One morning Mother Pig said,
"I wish I had room enough for you all to stay
and live with me forever, but, of course, I don't.
Today you must all go out into the world
and build houses of your own."
And so, the three little pigs ate a good breakfast,
kissed their mother good-bye,
and went off into the countryside.

The first little pig said, "I shall build my house of straw.
It will not take me very long, and then I'll have all the
rest of the day to eat and play and sleep."
He gathered a great heap of straw,
and in just a short time his house was finished.
So, he went inside, ate another breakfast,
played for a while with his new wooden top,
and then lay down in the corner for a cozy morning nap.

The second little pig said,
"I shall build my house of sticks.
I'll be done very quickly,
and then I can eat and play
and sleep all afternoon."
He collected a huge pile of sticks,
and in an hour or two his house
was finished.
He went inside, ate his lunch,
read some picture books until
he got sleepy, and then settled into
a chair for a comfy little snooze.

The third little pig said,
"I shall build my house of bricks and stones.
It will take me a long time,
but once it is finished, I will have a sturdy
house that is safe and beautiful."
All morning he gathered bricks and stones,
and all afternoon he worked and worked
to build his house.
When it was finally finished,
he went inside, locked the door,
ate a big dinner and then went right to bed.

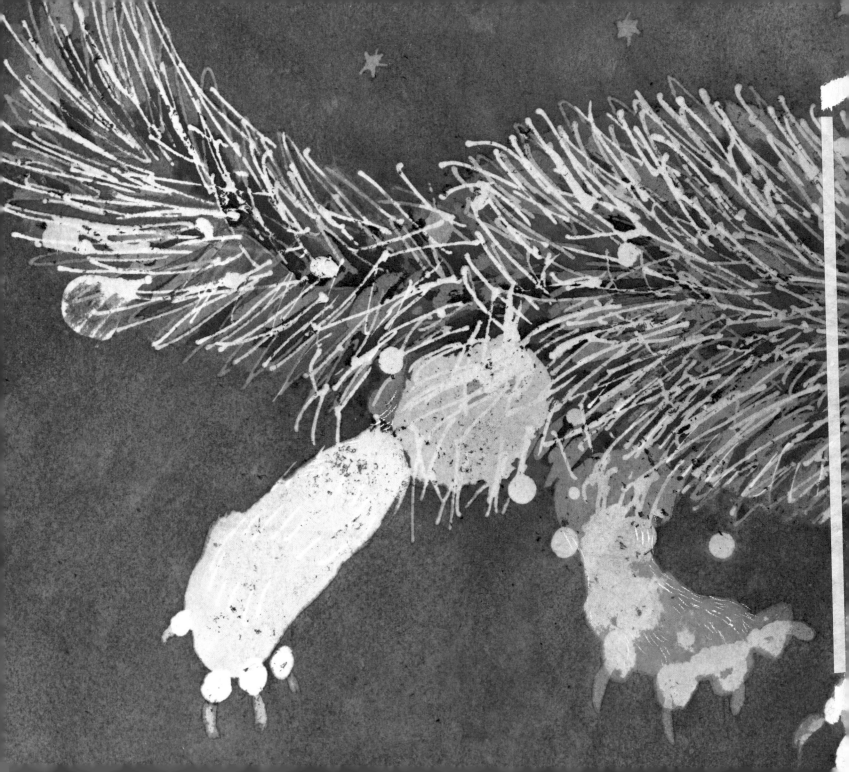

The wolf followed his nose,
and soon he was pounding on the door.
With a rowly growl he said,
"Little pigs, little pigs, let me come in!"
"Not by the hair of our chinny-chin-chins!"
answered the two frightened pigs.
The wolf said, "Very well then,
I shall huff, and I'll puff,
and I'll blow your house in!"
So he huffed and he puffed,
and he blew the house
into a big heap of sticks.
But when he searched for the plump
little pigs, he found nothing.

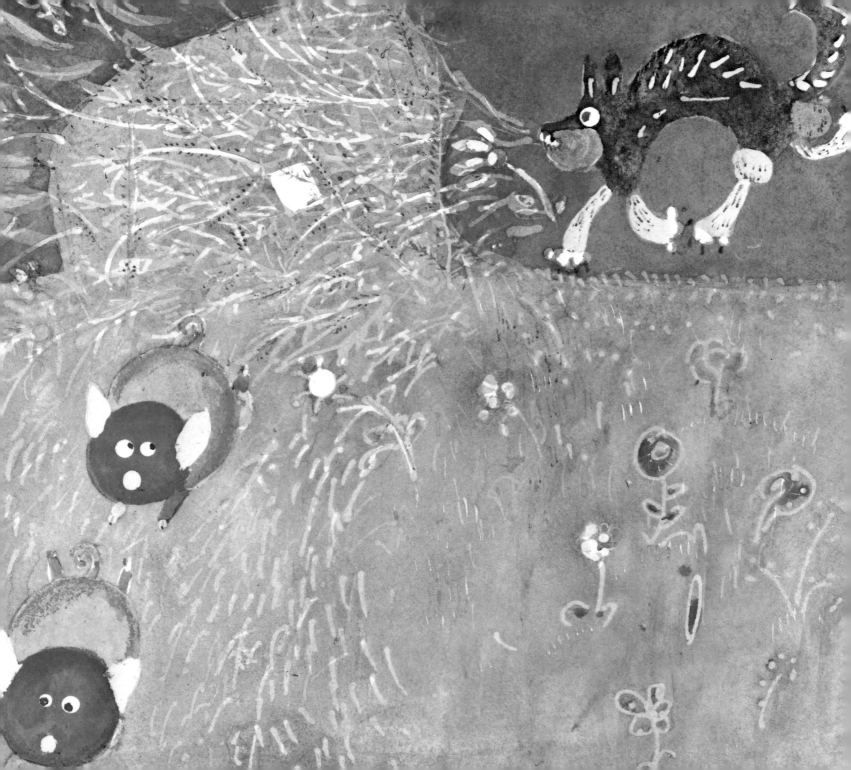

The two little pigs ran away
just as fast as their short chubby legs could carry them,
all the way to the brick and stone house of the third little pig.
Once inside, they locked the door,
and told the third little pig all about the big hungry wolf.

Before a minute had passed, the wolf was there,
beating on the door and shouting,
"Little pigs, little pigs, let me come in!"
"Not by the hair of our chinny-chin-chins!"
said the pigs from behind the stout oaken door.
"Then I'll huff and I'll puff, and I'll blow your house in!"
And the wolf huffed and he puffed and he blew a huge wind,
but the brick and stone house did not tumble down.

So he tried once again, with a mightier huff,
and a whooshier puff, and he blew and he blew,
but the house did not fall.
Now the wolf became angry,
and he scratched and he dug and he pounded and pushed,
and finally shouted,
"I will, yes, I WILL huff and puff and blow this house down!"
He started to huff, and he huffed and he huffed;
and then came the puffing, huge puff after puff;
and just when he started to blow down the house...

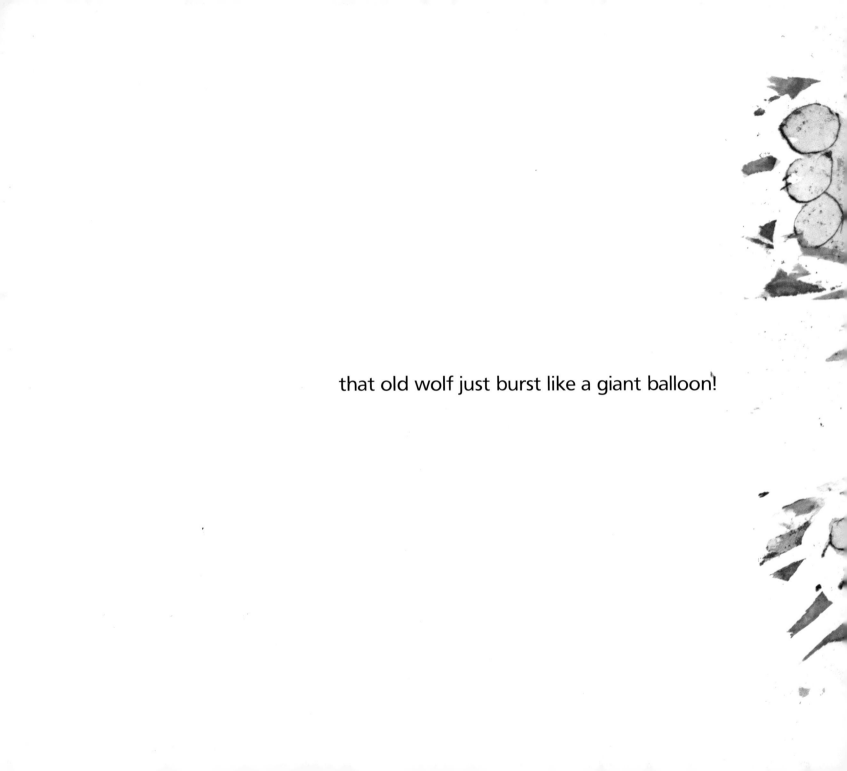

that old wolf just burst like a giant balloon!

When the three little pigs heard the huge noise,
they looked out and saw that the wolf was gone.
They squealed with joy, and danced and sang!

Then the three little pigs slept peacefully
for the rest of the night.

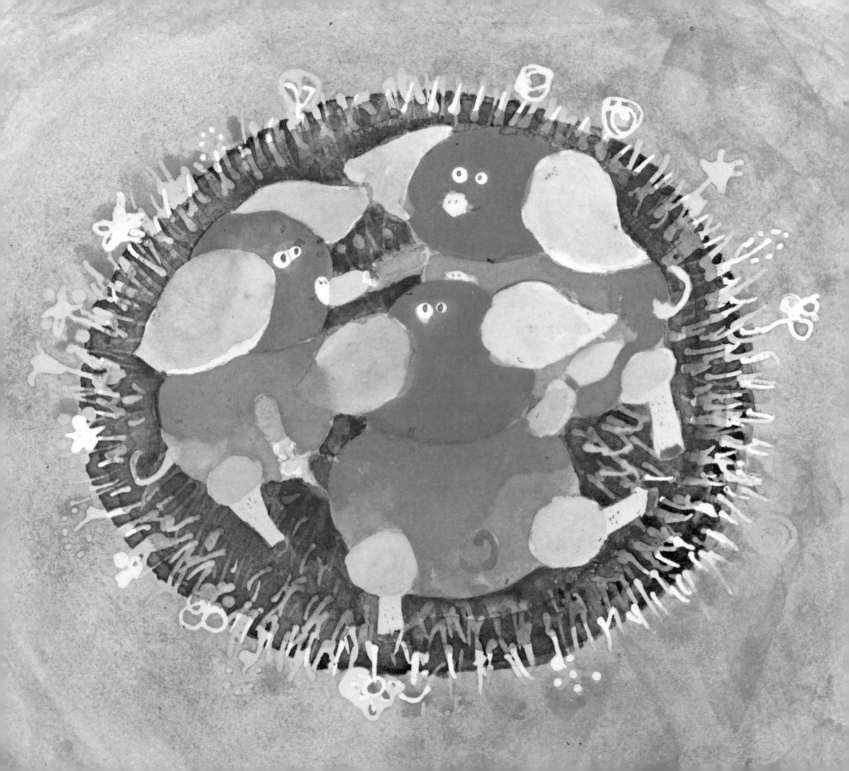

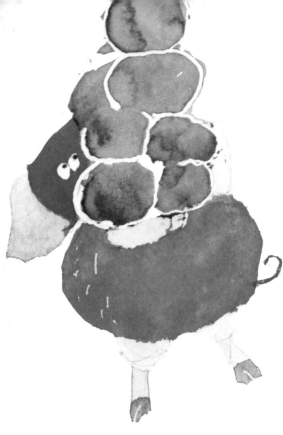

Bright and early the next morning, two little pigs
went to work and built themselves new houses —
not of straw,
and not of sticks,
but sturdy and beautiful little houses
made with bricks and stones.

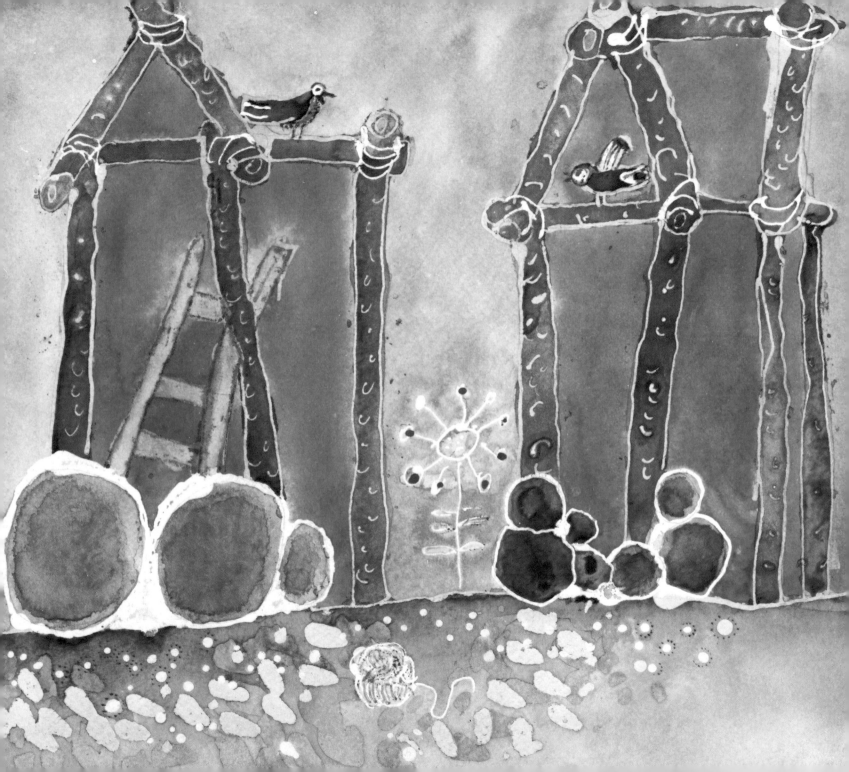

While the three little pigs slept
in their new houses, a hungry wolf
came stalking through the night.
"Snuff, snuff," he growled,
"I can smell a little pig!"

Knock, knock, went the wolf on the straw house door,
and he called, "Little pig, little pig, let me come in!"
"Not by the hair of my chinny-chin-chin!"
the first little pig replied. The old wolf said,
"Then I'll huff, and I'll puff, and I'll blow your house in!"
So he huffed and puffed and blew
until the house of straw collapsed.
But when he looked in the straw for his supper, it wasn't there.
The first little pig ran and ran,
and hid with the second little pig in the house of sticks.